Tadpoles
Fairytale Twists

The
Princess
and the
Frozen Peas

Written by Laura North

Illustrated by Joelle Dreidemy

Crabtree Publishing Company

www.crabtreebooks.com

Crabtree Publishing Company
www.crabtreebooks.com
1-800-387-7650

PMB 59051, 350 Fifth Ave.   616 Welland Ave.
59th Floor,   St. Catharines, ON
New York, NY 10118   L2M 5V6

Published by Crabtree Publishing in 2014

Series editor: Melanie Palmer
Editor: Crystal Sikkens
Notes to adults: Reagan Miller
Series advisor: Catherine Glavina
Series designer: Peter Scoulding
Production coordinator and
   Prepress technician: Margaret Amy Salter
Print coordinator: Margaret Amy Salter

Text © Laura North 2012
Illustrations © Joelle Dreidemy 2012

First published in 2012
by Franklin Watts
(A division of Hachette
Children's Books)

Printed in the
U.S.A./092014/CG20140808

Library and Archives Canada
Cataloguing in Publication

North, Laura, author
   The princess and the frozen peas / written by
Laura North ; illustrated by Joelle Dreidemy.

(Tadpoles: fairytale twists)
Issued in print and electronic formats.
ISBN 978-0-7787-0446-1 (bound).--ISBN 978-0-7787-
0481-2 (pbk.).--ISBN 978-1-4271-7566-3 (pdf).--ISBN
978-1-4271-7558-8 (html)

   I. Dreidemy, Joelle, illustrator II. Title.

PZ7.N815Pr 2014   j823'.92   C2013-908331-6
                                   C2013-908332-4

Library of Congress
Cataloging-in-Publication Data

CIP available at Library of Congress

This story is based on the traditional fairy tale,
The Princess and the Pea, but with a new twist.
Can you make up your own twist for the story?

There was once a young,
beautiful Princess who lived
in a huge kingdom.

One day, a very cranky, old king came to the royal palace intending to marry the Princess.

4

"Oh no" thought the Princess.
"I can't marry him!"

"The King wants proof that she's a real princess before he marries her," said one servant.

"A real princess won't be able to sleep if there is even only one tiny pea underneath a big pile of mattresses," said the other.

GRUMPF
GRUMPF

"I am a real princess," thought the Princess. "But I will pretend that I'm not."

The servants crept into her room and placed a single pea under her pile of mattresses.

"Oh, I am so sleepy," yawned the Princess and pretended to sleep.

The servants watched the Princess.
"Look! She's asleep already. The
King will be so angry!" cried one.

"Maybe one pea wasn't enough," said the other servant. "We must prove that she is a princess!"

The next night, they crept into her
room. "Lots of frozen peas should
do the trick!" they whispered.

"Oh, I am so terribly tired!"
said the Princess. She began
snoring loudly.

13

The next morning, she rose with the sun. "What a wonderful night's sleep I have had," the Princess smiled. The servants looked worried.

"But I really haven't slept a wink,"
thought the Princess, secretly.

The servants told the King
what had happened.

"What do you mean she's not a princess?" yelled the King. "Try harder!"

"Let's try other things that start with the letter P," said one servant.

"Good idea," said the other servant. "That's almost as good as a real pea."

19

The servants put some
prickly porcupines
into her bed.
But still the
Princess slept.

ZZ^Z

They tried a pirate...

and a panda...

a peacock...

...and a painter!

But still the Princess slept.

Soon it was the morning of the wedding. "She's not a princess," said the servants to the King. "Call the wedding off," sighed the King, and he left.

"Phew!" said the Princess. She didn't have to marry the old King. "And now," she said, "I can finally get a good night's sleep!"

Puzzle 1

Put these pictures in the correct order. Which event is the most important? Try writing the story in your own words. Use your imagination to put your own "twist" on the story!

Puzzle 2

1. The King gets very angry.

2. I want to marry a real princess.

3. I am so sleepy.

4. We must stop her from sleeping!

5. I have servants for everything.

6. I cannot marry that cranky, old King!

Match the speech bubbles to the correct character in the story. Turn the page to check your answers.

Notes for adults

TADPOLES: Fairytale Twists are engaging, imaginative stories designed for early fluent readers. The books may also be used for read-alouds or shared reading with young children.

TADPOLES: Fairytale Twists are humorous stories with a unique twist on traditional fairy tales. Each story can be compared to the original fairy tale, or appreciated on its own. Fairy tales are a key type of literary text found in the Common Core State Standards.

THE FOLLOWING PROMPTS BEFORE, DURING, AND AFTER READING SUPPORT LITERACY SKILL DEVELOPMENT AND CAN ENRICH SHARED READING EXPERIENCES:

1. **Before Reading:** Do a picture walk through the book, previewing the illustrations. Ask the reader to predict what will happen in the story. For example, ask the reader what he or she thinks the twist in the story will be.

2. **During Reading:** Encourage the reader to use context clues and illustrations to determine the meaning of unknown words or phrases.

3. **During Reading:** Have the reader stop midway through the book to revisit his or her predictions. Does the reader wish to change his or her predictions based on what they have read so far?

4. **During and After Reading:** Encourage the reader to make different connections:
   Text-to-Text: How is this story similar to/different from other stories you have read?
   Text-to-World: How are events in this story similar to/different from things that happen in the real world?
   Text-to-Self: Does a character or event in this story remind you of anything in your own life?

5. **After Reading:** Encourage the child to reread the story and to retell it using his or her own words. Invite the child to use the illustrations as a guide.

HERE ARE OTHER TITLES FROM TADPOLES: Fairytale Twists for you to enjoy:

Cinderella's Big Foot	978-0-7787-0440-9 RLB	978-0-7787-0448-5 PB
Jack and the Bean Pie	978-0-7787-0441-6 RLB	978-0-7787-0449-2 PB
Little Bad Riding Hood	978-0-7787-0442-3 RLB	978-0-7787-0450-8 PB
Princess Frog	978-0-7787-0443-0 RLB	978-0-7787-0452-2 PB
Sleeping Beauty—100 Years Later	978-0-7787-0444-7 RLB	978-0-7787-0479-9 PB
The Lovely Duckling	978-0-7787-0445-4 RLB	978-0-7787-0480-5 PB
The Three Little Pigs and the New Neighbor	978-0-7787-0447-8 RLB	978-0-7787-0482-9 PB

VISIT WWW.CRABTREEBOOKS.COM FOR OTHER CRABTREE BOOKS.

Answers
Puzzle 1
The correct order is: 1c, 2f, 3d, 4e, 5b, 6a
Puzzle 2
The Princess: 3, 6

The King: 2, 5

The servants: 1, 4